Neptune

Kate Riggs

CREATIVE EDUCATION
CREATIVE PAPERBACKS

seedlings

Published by Creative Education and Creative Paperbacks
P.O. Box 227, Mankato, Minnesota 56002
Creative Education and Creative Paperbacks
are imprints of The Creative Company
www.thecreativecompany.us

Design by Ellen Huber; production by Joe Kahnke
Art direction by Rita Marshall
Printed in the United States of America

Photographs by Alamy (Peter Horree), Black Cat Studios (RON
MILLER), Corbis (Mark Garlick Words & Pictures Ltd/Science
Photos Library), Getty Images (DETLEV VAN RAVENSWAAY/
SCIENCE PHOTO LIBRARY, Jason Reed, Stocktrek), NASA (NASA/
JPL), Science Source (Richard Bizley, John R. Foster, David Hardy),
Shutterstock (Diego Barucco, Here, Tristan3D)

Library of Congress Cataloging-in-Publication Data
Names: Riggs, Kate, author.
Title: Neptune / Kate Riggs.
Series: Seedlings.
Includes bibliographical references and index.
Summary: A kindergarten-level introduction to the planet
Neptune, covering its orbital process, its moons, and such
defining features as its dust rings, winds, and name.
Identifiers: ISBN 978-1-60818-917-5 (hardcover) / ISBN 978-1-
62832-533-1 (pbk) / ISBN 978-1-56660-969-2 (eBook)
This title has been submitted for CIP
processing under LCCN 2017938981.

CCSS: RI.K.1, 2, 3, 4, 5, 6, 7;
RI.1.1, 2, 3, 4, 5, 6, 7; RF.K.1, 3; RF.1.1

First Edition HC 9 8 7 6 5 4 3 2 1
First Edition PBK 9 8 7 6 5 4 3 2 1

TABLE OF CONTENTS

Hello, Neptune!

Neptune is the eighth planet from the sun. Bright-blue Neptune is cold. It is windy and icy there.

Winds on Neptune are strong. They are nine times stronger than Earth's!

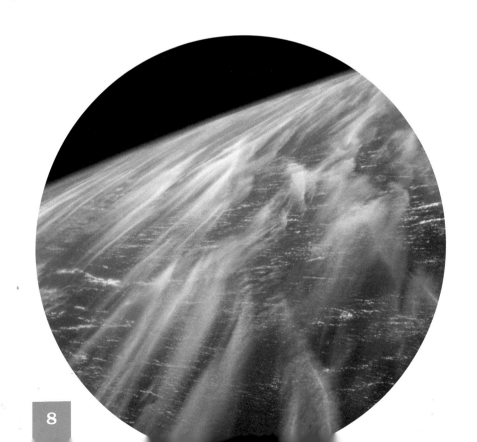

Six rings of dust circle Neptune. They are hard to see.

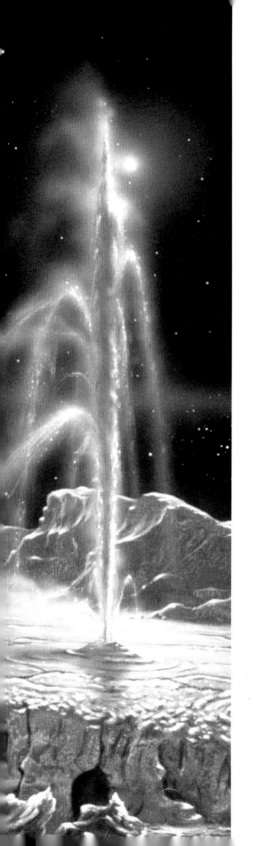

Thirteen moons
go around
Neptune. The
largest is named
Triton. There may
be a 14th moon.
It was first seen
in 2013.

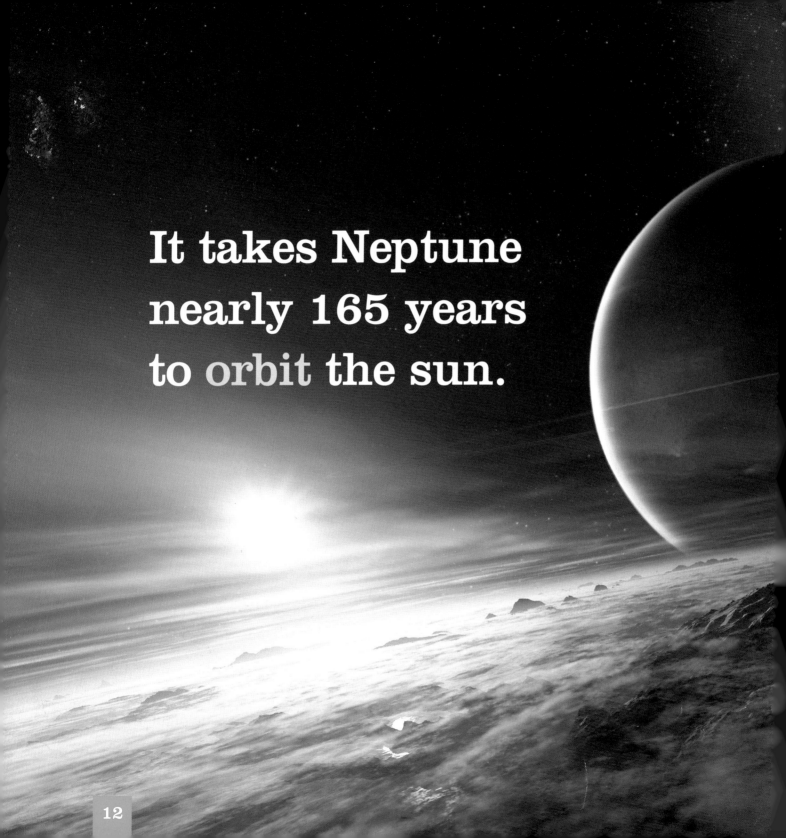

It takes Neptune
nearly 165 years
to orbit the sun.

Neptune is the
last planet in our
solar system.

Astronomers study planets.

They found Neptune in 1846. Neptune is named for an old story about the god of the sea.

Gases swirl. Winds push clouds across the planet.

Darkness is all around.

Goodbye, Neptune!

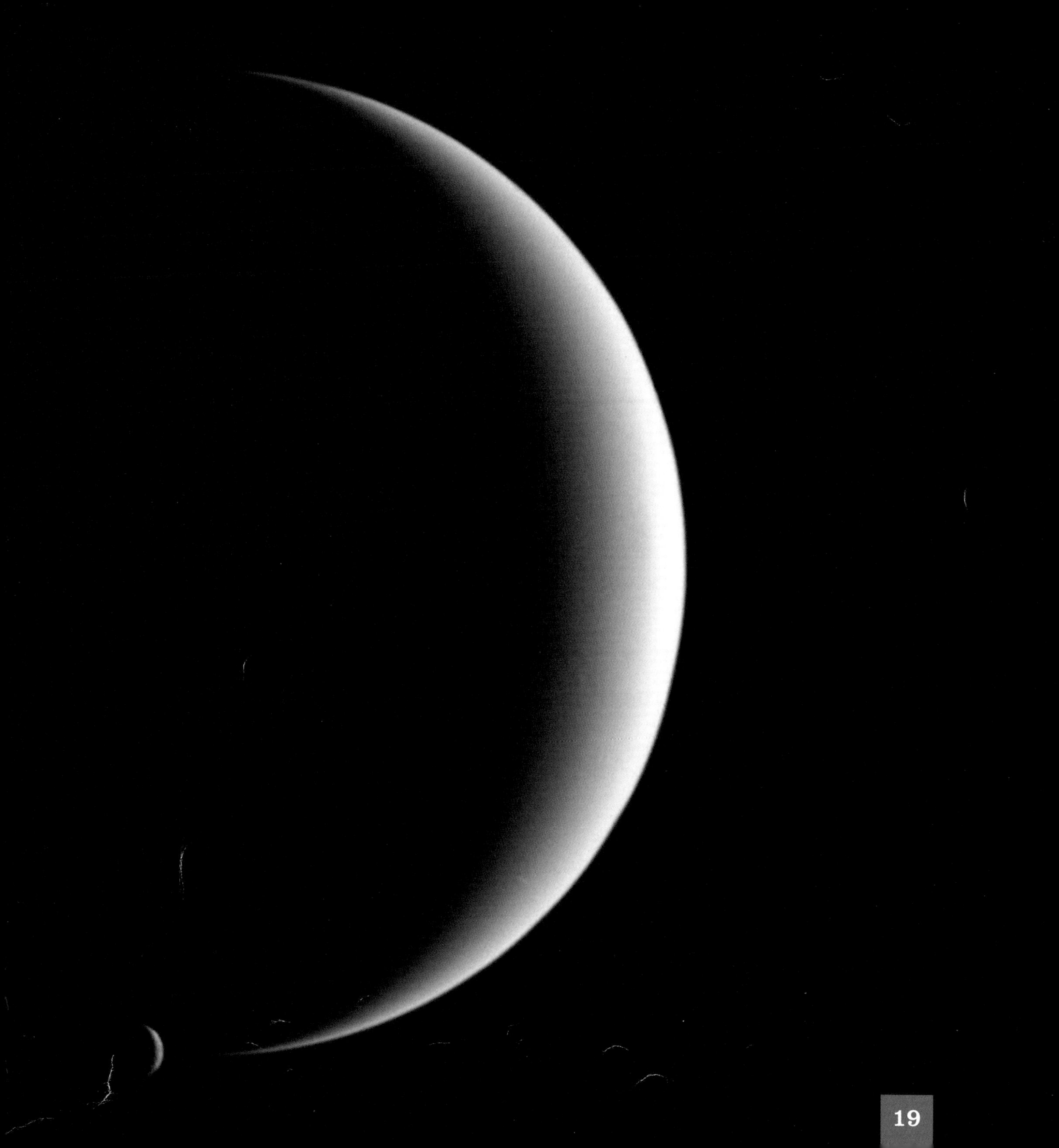

atmosphere

Great Dark Spot

rings

clouds

Triton

god: a being thought to have special powers and control over the world

orbit: the path a planet, moon, or other object takes around something else in outer space

planet: a rounded object that moves around a star

solar system: the sun, the planets, and their moons

Read More

Heos, Bridget. *Do You Really Want to Visit Neptune?* Mankato, Minn.: Amicus, 2014.

Loewen, Nancy. *Farthest from the Sun: The Planet Neptune.* Minneapolis: Picture Window Books, 2008.

Websites

NASA Jet Propulsion Laboratory: Kids
http://www.jpl.nasa.gov/kids/
Build a spacecraft or play a planetary game.

National Geographic Kids: Pluto's Secret
http://kids.nationalgeographic.com/games/adventure/plutos-secret/
Find out more about our solar system!

Index

Triton